Monday, Wednesday, and every other weekend

For Henry and Cooper
—K. S.

A FEIWEL AND FRIENDS BOOK
An Imprint of Macmillan

Library of Congress Cataloging-in-Publication Data Available

ISBN: 978-1-250-03489-2

The artwork was created with acrylic paint and collage on paper using old french math
pages, Italian hand-marbled paper scraps, shopping bags and Go Book pages from Japan,
antique Parisian wallpaper, tissue paper from a Chinese grocery, pages from old books
in french and Spanish, and travel guides and map parts from around the world.

Book design by April Ward

Feiwel and Friends logo designed by Filomena Tuosto

First Edition: 2014

2 4 6 8 10 9 7 5 3 1

mackids.com

Monday, Wednesday, And every otHer Weekend

kAren StantoN

FEIWEL AND FRIENDS ® NEW YORK

My name is Henry Cooper
and I live in two houses.
So does my dog, Pomegranate.

On Mondays, Wednesdays,
and every other weekend,
Pomegranate and I live with Mama
in apartment 3B on East Flower Street.

On Tuesdays, Thursdays, and every other weekend, Pomegranate and I live at Papa's house two and a half blocks away on West Woolsey Avenue.

In the mornings at Mama's apartment, the
hallways smell like chapati, tortillas, and miso
soup. Delicious words come floating through
the walls and into my open ears.

Mobiles hang from Mama's
ceiling, and they dance whenever
I walk by. Mama, Pomegranate,
and I dance, too.

In the evenings at Papa's house,
I read books in the poppy-red room
while Papa plays piano.

Sometimes, we all sing.
Especially Pomegranate.

And every other Saturday morning, I
eat Mama's perfect golden flapjacks while
Pomegranate barks at the window. "Sorry,
Pomegranate," I say. "No squirrels to chase
at Mama's house."

Pomegranate wants
to go home.

Every other Sunday night, I eat Papa's perfect pepperoni pizza in his tomato-red kitchen. The pizza is delicious, but Pomegranate's not hungry. He scratches at the back door and cries.

"Sorry, Pomegranate," I say.
"No place to dig for a digging
dog at Papa's house."

Pomegranate asks to go home.

My bedroom at Mama's house has a view
of the whole city. Even Mama's favorite food
truck, Mr. Bombay's Takeaway.

At Papa's house, I sleep under a ceiling painted with dragons in a magical forest. Pomegranate has his own special bed in both houses.

But tonight . . .

POMEGRANATE

When I get up in the morning,
Pomegranate is gone. I look for him
in the red rooms at Papa's house.

No Pomegranate.

Papa and I run to East Flower Street and call his name up and down the stairs with Mama. No Pomegranate.

"I'll check the pound," Papa says.

"I'll ask the neighbors," Mama says.

"You stay put," they both say.

But I can't stay put because I

think I know where he is.

I race down the block,

across the park,

and around
the corner

. . . to our old house.
The place where we all used
to live together.

And there is Pomegranate.

A little girl with yellow hair is petting Pomegranate. She smiles at me. She says her name is Penny and she wishes she had a dog just like Pomegranate.

I tell her I'm Henry and I push
her on the red swing that used
to be mine.

Shiny new wind chimes dance in
the tree above us like Mama's mobiles.
Tomatoes the same color as Papa's
kitchen grow in Penny's garden. I tell
Penny I have two new homes now.
And so does Pomegranate.

PENNYS
GARDIN

"Time to come inside now, Penny," her father calls.
And it's time for us to leave our old house behind.
"Come, Pomegranate," I say.

But Pomegranate
is not ready to go.

"It's okay,
Pomegranate,"
I say. "Follow me.

I'll show you

the way . . .

back home."

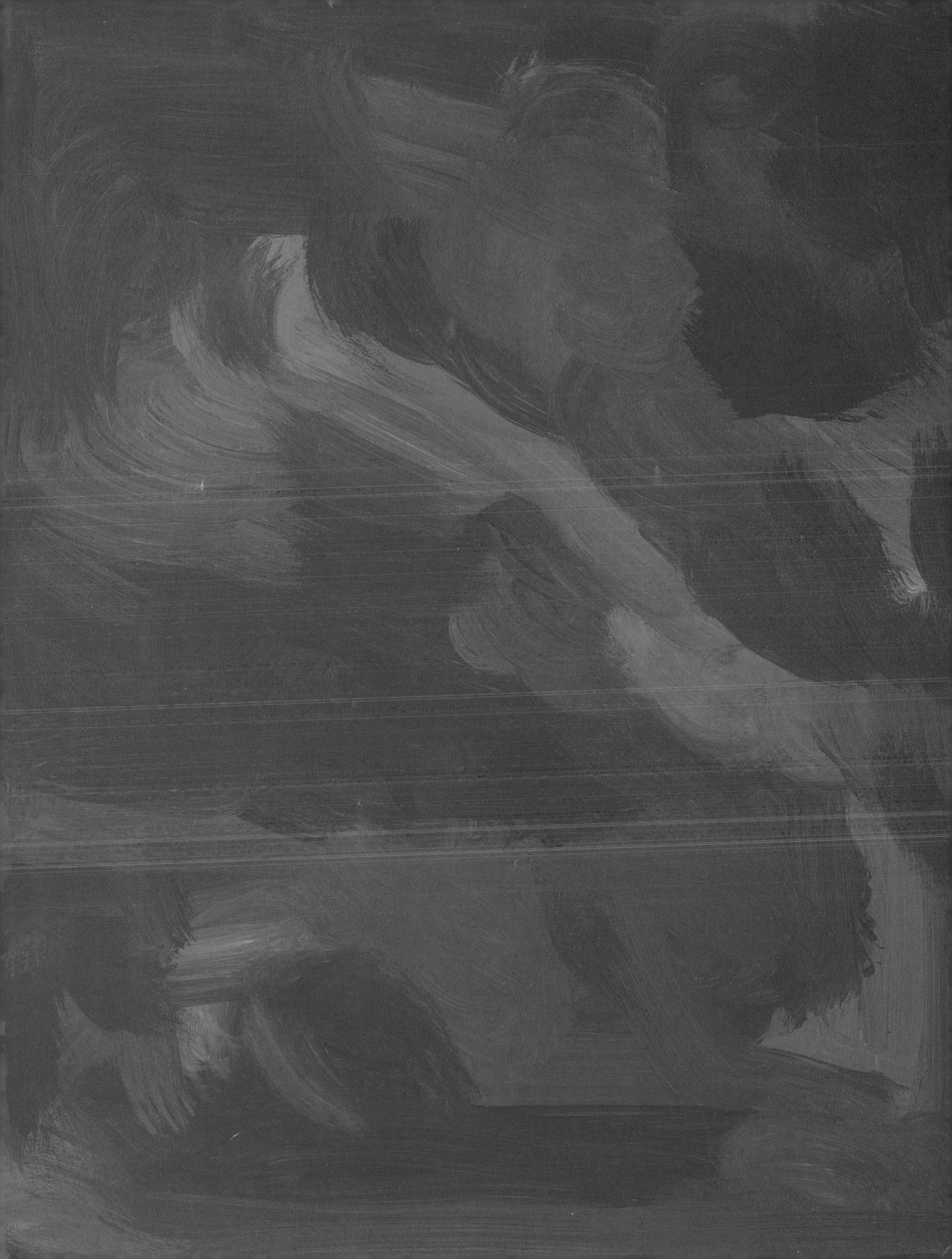